Mia's life

Sister Disaster

OTHER FUN MIA'S LIFE STORIES!

Fan Takeover

Best Friends for Never

Mia's Life

Sister Disaster

SOCIAL MEDIA STAR
Mia Fizz

sourcebooks
young readers

Cover illustration by Stephanie Yue
Internal illustrations by Lidia Fernandez Abril
Cover design by Maryn Arreguín/Sourcebooks
Internal design by Ashley Holstrom/Sourcebooks

The characters and events portrayed in this book are fictitious or are used fictitiously. Any similarity to real persons, living or dead, is purely coincidental and not intended by the author.

Published by Sourcebooks Young Readers, an imprint of Sourcebooks
P.O. Box 4410, Naperville, Illinois 60567–4410
(630) 961-3900
sourcebooks.com

Cataloging-in-Publication Data is on file with the Library of Congress

Source of Production: Versa Press, East Peoria, Illinois, United States
Date of Production: March 2022
Run Number: 5024721

Printed and bound in the United States of America.
VP 10 9 8 7 6 5 4 3 2 1

1

"Watch out!"

I turned around just in time to see a girl on a skateboard heading right for me. I dodged out of the way as she zoomed past, her blond curls flying behind her.

"Sorry!" she shouted.

"No worries! Hair goals!" I called after her, and she shot me a thumbs-up.

"Woah. Close call," my BFF, Briony, said. She sat on a bench outside the community center scrolling TikTok while I paced. My little sister Sienna was going to get out of space camp soon, and we were waiting to take her to go get ice cream at a new vegan café. It was one of those perfect spring days where the sun was shining but it wasn't *too* warm, so we'd headed outside instead of lounging on the couches indoors.

"I know. I have to pay better attention." The truth is, I was a massive klutz. Getting run into by a rogue skateboarder wouldn't exactly have been surprising. But my klutziness was part of what drew people to my YouTube channel, *Mia's Life*. I didn't try to hide any of the awkward things in life, and it helped others get through their own awkward moments. I created videos on everything from periods to pimples to painting.

Just then, though, my brain had gone completely AWOL. "I was totally daydreaming," I admitted.

The community center wasn't *just* for space camps—it was where I'd met my crush, Finn, at a rock-climbing class. I hadn't hung out with him in a while, and I was trying to think of the perfect text to send. Maybe something asking him to hang out or making a joke? I couldn't decide.

SPACE CAMP
Adventure awaits

I wondered if I should ask the Miacorns—the millions of people who tuned into my channel—but I decided against it. After all, I was trying hard to keep *some* aspects of my life off the web, and Finn was definitely one of them. At least for now.

Then my eye caught on something bright pink on the bulletin board hanging outside the center.

"Briony, did you see this?" I reached up and pulled the flyer down.

"Um, I don't think you're supposed to take those down," Briony said.

"I'll put it right back! Come see!"

She hopped off her bench and came over. I excitedly shoved the piece of paper in her face.

Briony frowned, her brown hair falling into her eyes. "A...cheesy graphic of a crown?"

"Read the *words*, Briony!" I laughed. "A dance! A real dance, right here at the community center!"

Suddenly, I thought of every movie I'd ever seen

with a school dance. I'd always wished I could go to one, but my sister and I were homeschooled. So it was unlikely. It's not like the Fizz family was going to rent out a gym and put some punch out on a table for me and Sienna to rock out! But dances just seemed so magical. The lights, the music, the amazing dresses...and the potential for a cute boy on my arm.

"Oh, fun!" Briony said. "I've only been to one dance at our school, and it was a blast. It was an 'Under the Sea' theme, and the dance committee decorated the entire gym like the ocean. I felt like a mermaid all night!"

"It looks like this one is themed like a royal ball," I said excitedly. "That's so cute! Very royalcore."

"*And*," Briony said, raising her eyebrows, "it would make a good vlog."

"Totally," I said. Thinking up content ideas for my YouTube channel came super naturally to me. I could get a ton of videos out of the dance—everything from a shopping haul to tips on getting ready to makeup tutorials. Maybe I could get into the dance early and even do a behind-the-scenes look at the decorations. Plus, if I made a vlog out of it, I'd always have the memories to look back on. Just like one of those cheesy home videos parents made of their kids in movies right before they headed off to prom!

"You're coming with me, right?" I said. "It's next weekend! I can't go by myself."

"Sure," Briony said. "I'll ask my parents for permission, but I'm pretty sure we don't have any plans. It's definitely something different than the average Saturday night. I mean, you know the closest I get to *actually* dancing is binge-watching *Dance Moms*, but a royal ball idea is too cute. We should do big ball gowns!"

I texted a photo of the flyer to my mom, asking if I could go. She quickly responded with a thumbs-up sign and said that it looked like fun. The plan was on.

"Let's make a list of what we have to do," I said, getting super excited. I whipped out my phone and opened up my Notes app. We needed to buy tickets, find dresses, do our nails, check Pinterest for cute royalcore ideas, and test out makeup looks. I couldn't wait for Sienna to get out of camp so we could get started. My sister helped with my channel sometimes, too. She was like Briony—both of them simultaneously reminded me to keep things authentic and pushed me out of my comfort zone.

"Oh, I have an idea of something you could do," said Briony. "Not only would it make an *amazing* video, but I think you'll have a lot of fun doing it."

"What?" I asked.

My BFF grabbed my phone, quickly typing something into it. I recognized the smirk on her face. Briony was up to something!

When she handed my phone back, I saw what she had written in all caps. My heart dropped to the floor.

ASK FINN TO THE DANCE!

2

"Absolutely not," I said instantly, handing my phone back. "Delete, delete, delete."

"Why?" Briony cried. "Don't tell me you've turned into one of those girls who think only *boys* can be the ones to give dance invitations. That's not the Mia Fizz I know!"

"Um, of *course* not," I said. "But...I can't ask Finn. We haven't talked in a while. And besides..."

"Besides what?" Briony asked, bumping her shoulder into mine. "Besides, he's nice, adorable, fun to be around, and understanding about your career. Besides, you were just telling me how much you've enjoyed getting to know him."

"What if he says no?" I asked quietly.

That was what I was *really* afraid of. How awkward it would feel to get rejected. If he did say no, I could probably never speak to him again. As opposed to now, when I could mainly live in my daydreams, I would feel like such a loser. What if he laughed about me with his friends?

"Mia," said Briony, shaking her head. "Come on. First of all, I doubt he'll say no. If he didn't have a crush on you back, he wouldn't have come to Sienna's birthday party or to the play you helped me with! So what if he *does* say no? Who cares? That's literally the worst thing that could happen, and you'd be fine. We'd eat some ice cream, pretend we didn't know him, and never speak of it again. Then we'd go to the dance and have fun! It's not like you *need* a date to go. Lots of people at my school go to dances with groups of friends. I didn't have a date to the Under the Sea dance, and I still had a great time."

I had to admit, Briony was making sense. Finn wasn't the kind of guy who would go around talking about me negatively. And if I was embarrassed...so what? Life was full of embarrassing moments. I mean, hadn't I almost been knocked over by a curly-haired skateboarder five seconds ago? I would deal.

"And," said Briony, "I think you should share it with the Miacorns."

I gulped. "You do?"

"Yes. You want to show them the *real* Mia Fizz, don't you? Not just the perfectly filtered version, but your ups and your downs. The moments when you're brave."

"You make it sound like I'm about to jump out of an airplane."

"Been there, done that, remember?" Briony asked. We both laughed—I'd done a skydiving video a couple of years ago. It had been one of the coolest videos I'd ever made!

"I mean, this *is* scarier than jumping out of a plane,

if I'm being honest," I said. "At least, my heart's beating faster now than it was then."

"And this is such a common thing! School dances, yeah, but, also, just girls being nervous to send guys a text," Briony pointed out. "It's so relatable. I know there are some things you like to keep private, and that's important. But this is such a major moment for you. When *you* have courage, it gives the Miacorns courage. You can demonstrate how to do something you're terrified of doing. If he says no, we'll go to the dance anyway and have the night of our lives! Deal?"

I bit my lip. I knew my BFF was right, but I could still feel the palms of my hands getting sweaty. Ever since I'd met Finn, I hadn't been able to stop thinking about him. He was someone I knew I could have a lot of fun with at the dance, and it would make the entire experience that much more special. After all, in all of those movies about dances, the girl usually had a fabulous date.

Plus, he'd look *so* cute in a suit.

I took my phone back from Briony and glanced at the time. Sienna was going to be done with space camp any minute. What were the chances I'd gather up the nerve later, when I was home all by myself? Not very high.

"All right, can you film me?" I asked Briony.

She nodded and pulled out her phone. She'd helped me film content for my channel tons of times before, so she knew exactly what to do.

I took a deep breath and started talking to the camera. "Hi, Miacorns! I'm about to do something that's really scary for me, and I thought it was worth sharing with you. I'm going to ask a boy that I like to go to a dance with me. I've never asked someone out before, and I honestly feel like I'm shaking! But I also think it's important to try to be brave with these kinds of things, and, whatever happens, I hope it encourages you to be brave, too. Here we go..."

Before I could change my mind, I pulled up Finn's

contact info. I took a quick photo of the flyer for the dance and shot it his way.

Hey...free next weekend? If so, I know a girl who would love to go to this dance with you! Her name's Mia and she's a rock-climbing newbie...ring any bells?

I held my phone and stared at it. He probably wouldn't even see the message anytime soon. He could be doing homework or hanging out with his brother or...

OMG.

Those three little dots!

He was responding!

3

That sounds fun—I'm in!

"OMG!" I squealed, holding my phone up to Briony and her camera. "He said yes!"

Briony shrieked and paused the recording so we could jump up and down. People were probably looking at us, but I couldn't have cared less. It was really happening. I was going to a dance—with the boy of my dreams!

"Why are you two so excited?" Sienna appeared suddenly, her hair falling out of her long brown ponytail.

"We're going to a dance next weekend here at the community center," I explained.

"*And*," Briony butted in, "Finn said that he would go as Mia's date!"

Sienna's jaw dropped. "You have a *date*? Like, a real, live date? Do you think he'll get you a corsage? Will you kiss? What's he going to wear? What are *you* going to wear? Will you rent a limo? What about—"

"Okay, okay," I laughed. "I need ice cream to answer all of these questions!"

"Same here," Briony said. "Let's go!"

The three of us headed to the café, chatting the entire time about the dance. After we got three vegan strawberry sundaes, we sat outside at a cute picnic table covered by an awning and started strategizing. Sienna, like Briony and I, had seen plenty of movies about school dances.

"First things first," said Sienna, licking her spoon. "What are you going to do about a dress? It has to be something really special."

"No idea," I admitted. "I don't really have anything that screams *dance*." I thought through my closet, but nothing came to mind. I didn't usually wear things

that were super formal or fancy—my favorite outfits consisted of a cute crop top and a pair of distressed jeans. After all, I spent most of my time hanging out with my family, traveling, doing school, painting, or making YouTube videos. Nothing that required a sparkly, special outfit!

"Well, we'll have to go shopping," said Briony. "I'm sure we can find something that screams *cute* and *royal*. And Finn will think you look gorgeous no matter what."

I grinned, picturing how much fun we were going to have. I was so caught up in my excitement that I almost forgot to snag photos of our ice cream and tag the café. I always tried to share with the Miacorns where you could get great treats that tasted good *and* didn't harm any animals. I quickly snapped a Boomerang clip of the three of us showing off our sundaes.

Soon enough, Mom pulled up in front of the café to pick us up and gave a quick honk. The three of us hopped into the car, and I gave quick kisses to my youngest siblings, Karma and Koa, who were strapped into their car seats. As soon as we were buckled, I turned to Mom.

"So, I have big news," I told her excitedly.

"The new café's ice cream is delicious?" Mom asked.

"Well, yes. We definitely need to go back. But also—"

"Finn is going to the dance as her date!" Sienna cried from the back seat.

"Sienna!" I laughed. "Spoiler alert!" But I couldn't even be that annoyed with my sister. I knew she was just happy for me.

"Wow, Mia!" Mom's eyes widened. "That's a big deal!"

I shrugged, trying to play it cool. "I sent him a text asking him to go, and he said yes."

"Don't let her convince you she played it cool," Briony said, leaning forward between me and my mom. "She was totally having a freak-out about it."

I rolled my eyes, but Mom chuckled. "Well, I'm sure it was nerve-racking. But that's terrific. Finn seems like such a nice guy. And I'm really, really proud of you for having the courage to ask him to the dance! That's a big deal."

"Thanks, Mom," I said. My mom and I had always

been really close. She'd had me when she was only a teenager, so she still remembered things like what it was like to go to a school dance. Besides, we'd talked about dating and guys a million times. We'd even filmed some of our conversations for YouTube. We didn't keep secrets from each other. I knew she'd be in my corner.

"The only problem is, I have nothing to wear," I said.

"Well, that's an easy fix," Mom said with a grin. "Sounds like a shopping trip is in order! You could make an entire vlog out of it. Maybe the Miacorns could help you pick your dress. I'm sure they'd love to follow along."

I nodded. "I already have all of these video ideas about getting ready for a dance. I want to include them every step of the way. Most of them have probably already been to a dance, though. *They* might need to be teaching *me* this time around." That was how I felt about my viewers—they were like my friends, not just random internet strangers.

"I promise we'll make a trip to the mall happen this week," Mom said.

BFF? Check. Boy? Check. Plan for a dress? Check. I'd gone from zero to totally excited in only an hour. I reread Finn's text and took a screenshot this time. I wanted to keep that message forever!

4

That night, after dinner, I was preparing to make a YouTube video to tell the Miacorns about the dance when Sienna burst into my room.

"Okay, I've been mood-boarding," she said. "I think I have some awesome dance looks for you. You're going to be the coolest girl there."

"Ooh, perfect! Let me see!" I grabbed her phone. Sienna loved being involved in my channel. In fact, she came up with the idea for me to interact with my Instagram followers more and let them choose different dares for me. If she hadn't convinced me to do a fan takeover, I never would have met Finn! She had her own Instagram profile and YouTube channel that my parents helped her run. She was almost like my little assistant sometimes.

I took a look at the screen. Sienna had gone above and beyond. Not only had she created a Pinterest board—Mia's Dance—but she'd made other boards nested inside it. There was one for my hair, one for my makeup, and one for my dress.

"This is amazing, Sienna! Thanks!" I excitedly opened the one for my hair, and...

Well.

Didn't *love* it.

Okay, I *hated* it! Most of the photos were totally wacky.

"Pink hair?" I asked, scrunching my nose a little bit.

"OMG, yeah. You can do it with Kool Aid! I've seen a thousand TikToks about it," Sienna said happily.

I kept scrolling. There was a lot of Kool Aid hair dye and elaborate updos that looked like they'd take ages. They screamed *Shadow and Bone* more than community center dance.

Well, her vision for my hair didn't exactly match mine. But maybe her makeup looks would be better—Sienna and I loved playing around with makeup together. She definitely had a good sense of what I liked there.

I clicked over onto the makeup board. There was photo after photo of way over-the-top makeup looks. There were *tons* of sparkles, rhinestones, and bright colors.

"I'm not sure if..." I trailed off.

Sienna shook her head. "Trust me, Mia! It's a *dance*. You can't just wear your everyday look. You need to take things to the next level of glam."

"I mean, I wasn't going to just wear my natural, daily makeup. I thought maybe a brighter lip gloss color, though, not...turquoise eyeshadow." I couldn't imagine telling the Miacorns that *these* looks were what I was going to create for a dance. There was no way.

Sienna rolled her eyes. "Well, look at the dress board."

I hesitantly clicked over to the board she'd made on dresses. And, just like I'd been dreading, she'd pinned some really out-there gowns that just weren't me. They weren't necessarily *bad*, but they were feathered and huge with weird cutouts and all shades of the rainbow. One had a sparkling unicorn made of gemstones on the front. One had *wings*. Nothing looked like a princess gown, at all.

I looked at Sienna. She was so hopeful, and I knew she really wanted to be part of the entire experience. She was too young to go to the dance, so this was the next best thing for her. I couldn't break her heart by telling her how much I didn't like her Pinterest boards. Even though—*wings? Really, Sienna?*

"Thanks," I told her meekly. "These look great."

"I know, right?" she beamed. "I knew I could help! You'll look so beautiful, Finn won't believe how lucky he is."

Aww. I had the sweetest sister. I didn't know what to say, but I knew I couldn't tell her that she was all wrong.

"Thanks, Sienna. Let's look at these more tomorrow. I have some work to do before bed," I told her.

"Good night!" she chirped, skipping out of my room.

As soon as the door closed behind her, I groaned. Great. How could I tell Sienna I wasn't inspired at all by her hard work? Or should I just grin and bear it and let her take the lead? Maybe she was right. Was I not thinking big enough about my look? Was I just trying to be comfortable again?

I turned on my camera to try and make a YouTube video, but I couldn't think of anything to say. I was too worried about Sienna's feelings. I reached over and turned the camera back off. Maybe I'd try again tomorrow. Or maybe this whole dance idea wasn't so great after all.

There was a knock on my door, and Dad poked his head in.

"Hey, Mia," he said. "You heading to bed soon?"

I nodded, but he instantly knew something was wrong.

"What's going on?" he asked. "You look...not like yourself."

I sighed. "That's part of the problem."

He came in, shutting the door behind him. "What do you mean?"

I explained about Sienna and her Pinterest boards.

"It's hard to trust my instincts," I admitted. I didn't know if I really *did* need to try and think outside the box or if I should be more confident about what *I* wanted to wear.

The dance was important to me. It wasn't just that I wanted to look cute for Finn—I wanted to look cute for myself! If I was wearing something that I didn't feel confident in, I knew I'd be distracted and self-conscious instead of having fun. And I always tried to be my most authentic self for my viewers. The same way I wouldn't wear something unusual just because a brand sent it to me, I couldn't wear something wacky just because my sister wanted me to. It wouldn't be me.

Dad nodded as I told him all of this.

"I totally understand," he said. "Remember, your sister's just excited. You know how much she looks up to you. She wants to be a part of your channel, and you've always been so great at letting her help. But, at the end of the day, Sienna is Sienna and you are you. You don't need to try to be anybody else. You should look how *you* want to look for the dance and just be honest with Sienna. There are plenty of other ways she can help, like with filming vlogs or even helping you get ready. I bet, if you put your heads together, you can come up with some fantastic ideas."

I sighed. I knew my dad was probably right. I just had to sit Sienna down and explain to her that the looks she had in mind weren't right for me.

But I knew it wasn't going to be easy.

5

I decided to wait until the next morning. Maybe after a good night's beauty sleep, Sienna would detach a little from her Pinterest plans. And maybe *I* would feel less anxious about talking to her after I got some shut-eye.

When I came downstairs, still in my favorite pink pajamas, Dad and Sienna were cutting up some fruit to have for breakfast. I slid into a seat at the kitchen table and yawned.

"Up all night dreaming about the big dance?" Mom asked, scooping some yogurt into Koa's mouth.

I smiled weakly. "Kind of." Actually, I'd been tossing and turning, thinking about what I would say to Sienna. *And* what I'd wear to the dance!

"I showed her all of my ideas last night," Sienna said excitedly, popping a piece of kiwi into her mouth.

"Great," Mom responded. "Hopefully you got some ideas for a dress!"

"Briony and I made plans to go shopping this afternoon," I told Mom. "I'm sure we'll find *something*."

"That sounds great. I can drop you off at the mall once Briony's school day is over. And, speaking of school, what are you girls up to for schoolwork today?"

Mom and Dad gave us free rein when it came to our homeschooling. I learned a ton from running *Mia's Life*—math, marketing strategy, analytics, and art. I also had a Spanish tutor I met with over Skype, and I kept up with a reading list for English. I exercised regularly for gym class, and Sienna and I liked doing fun science experiments we found online. Our family's travels were a great way to learn social studies, history, and geography. We loved checking out cool museums and new places. Homeschooling wasn't for everyone, but it was definitely the right fit for us! Especially when Briony told me about things like mystery meat in the cafeteria or dissecting a frog in biology class.

"Mia, can you help me with my Spanish homework today?" Sienna asked. "If I go back to my tutor and tell her and I still don't have my colors memorized, I'm worried she's going to make me switch to Latin instead."

I laughed. "Sure thing." That would be the perfect time to have a chat with her about her dance ideas.

After breakfast, I quickly got ready for the day, running through what I was going to say to my sister over and over in my head. When I knocked on Sienna's door, she was hunched over her laptop, looking frustrated.

"Hi," I said. "Or should I say, *hola*."

She groaned. "Spanish is so impossible. I'm just not good at it."

"Hey," I told her. "That's no way to talk about yourself!

It may not come *naturally* to you right this second. But, the more you practice, the better you'll get."

Sienna sighed, twirling the end of her brown braid with her finger. "I guess."

"Actually...Before we go over *los colores*, I was hoping to talk to you about the dance," I told her.

She grinned. "Now, *that* sounds more fun! Did you take a closer look at my mood boards?"

"Well, actually...Sienna, I really appreciate you putting all that time into helping me think of a look. I can tell you worked so hard on those Pinterest boards. But they just don't really feel like *me*. I know you want to help me try new things and think outside the box, but I also want to feel like myself, especially since it's my first real date. I don't want to feel like I'm wearing a costume or pretending to be something I'm not. I want to feel beautiful *and* comfortable. You know?"

"I guess I know what you mean," she admitted.

Relief flowed through me—she understood!

"I just got super excited," she continued, "and maybe a little ahead of myself. I thought you'd want to really stand out. But I know that *you're* the one going to the dance, and *you* should pick how you look. Besides, I think some of those hairstyles would take us hours."

"Or a professional," I said.

"Or a miracle," she added.

We giggled, and I threw my arm around her shoulders. "You know I appreciate you though, right? And I *do* want your help!"

"Duh," said Sienna jokingly. "And you need it! Maybe after you help me with Spanish, we could look on Pinterest *together*. That way, I can help you, but you can tell me what's a hit or what's a miss."

"Deal," I said. We could count it as art class—after all, putting together an awesome look dealt a lot with colors, angles, and creativity. It was the perfect homeschooling project.

We ran through the colors in Spanish together. I loved learning Spanish. When we traveled somewhere that was mainly Spanish-speaking, I felt way more confident knowing the language! Sienna wasn't as bad at it as she thought—she just needed a little help with memorization. I taught her some of my best tricks, like how *blanco* sounded like "blank," and a blank sheet of paper is white.

"Okay, I think I got this," said Sienna.

"Pop quiz. What's the color of my shirt?" I asked her.

"Um...*rosa?*"

"Perfect! Yours?"

"*Azul.*" She pointed to her navy sweatshirt, which had a glittery cat on the front of it.

I high-fived her. "See? It just takes practice."

"Speaking of practice..." she pulled up Pinterest on her laptop. "Let's take a break and find some looks for the dance, because we're probably going to have to practice your hairstyle this week!"

Sienna and I scrolled through the endless hair and makeup inspo pics. There were tons of options, even when we narrowed it down to "royal ball looks." We finally realized that there were things we both liked—gentle curls, dainty tiaras, and royal red lips.

"What about this?" asked Sienna. She pulled up a photo of a girl with large, bouncing, blond curls.

"That's so cute!" I squealed. The model's curly

do reminded me of the skateboarder who'd almost knocked me over at the community center. She looked like a glamorous princess.

But the look also made me nervous. My hair was stick-straight. I usually wore it in long braids. I didn't mind my hair—I loved its sunshiny blond color, and having straight hair meant it was pretty easy to take care of. But I hardly ever tried to curl it. I wasn't even sure if it could hold curls. And, if it could, would they just flatten? Or would they be *too* huge and make me look like a poodle? Would my hair get in my face if I tried to dance? What if it got caught in my lip gloss or something equally embarrassing? What if Finn didn't like it?

"It's still kind of out there for me," I admitted. "But I really like it. I think I want to try it."

"Yay!" said Sienna. "We can practice this week. Don't worry about a thing—you're going to look amazing. We've got this."

I pushed my worries away and smiled. Sienna was probably right. If my hair didn't look the way I wanted, I could always just wear it straight. What could go wrong?

6

On the way to the mall that afternoon, I filled Mom and Briony in on my conversation with Sienna. I also told them I'd made a vlog that afternoon about the dance and asking Finn out. People were so excited for me, and, now that I'd smoothed things out with Sienna, the excitement was getting to me, too! I'd already made a list of the videos I wanted to make—a *getting ready* vlog, a *how to do your makeup for a dance* vlog, and a recap vlog after I got home. The Miacorns would be with me every step of the way.

"It sounds like it went really well," Mom said. "You told her the truth, and she got what you were saying."

"I think so," I responded. "I feel relieved. I *want* her to be a part of my channel." I knew some people didn't really get along with their little sisters, and, sure, Sienna and I argued sometimes. What siblings didn't? But, at the end of the day, my family was incredibly close. I wanted Sienna to always know how much I loved being her big sis.

"Well, I love the hairstyle you guys landed on," said Briony. "It's so princessy!"

"That's what I thought, too," I said. "Now, if only my hair can handle it!"

"I'm sure your curls will be able to make it through a dance," Briony assured me. "Think of all the celebrities who have to rock fancy hairdos on red carpets and at movie premieres for hours!"

"Hair spray helps," Mom pointed out. "We'll just have to go to town."

"Nobody better light any flames near me," I said, and we all cracked up.

"I think I'm going to do a braided updo kind of thing," Briony said, showing me a photo on her phone.

"*So* cute," I told her. "Will you be able to do it yourself?"

"I'm going to try and practice it tonight," she said. "And I'm going to get a haircut first. But, today, we have to focus on finding the right dresses."

Mom pulled into the mall parking lot and unlocked the doors. "I'll be right back here in two hours. You girls have fun!"

As Briony and I headed into one of our favorite shops, she said, "So, for a royal feel, we need to find ball gowns with big skirts. And some tulle or something shimmery, preferably."

I nodded. "Let's get to looking!"

After digging through the racks of dresses, we found a few that we thought would work. Briony fell in love with hers instantly—it was an emerald green that would look perfect with her skin tone. She looked incredible in it.

Briony was always good at making decisions while

shopping. She knew what she liked and what she didn't almost instantly!

I, however, couldn't decide. I found dresses that fit our criteria: one that was blue with a white and gold overlay, one that was a shimmery pink tulle with delicate stars on top, and one that was a golden color with silver feathers sewn into it. They all felt appropriate to me.

"I love the pink, but do you think I wear *too* much pink?" I mused.

"It's your favorite," said Briony thoughtfully. "But you do wear it a lot. Maybe something different for the dance would make it feel more special?"

"I can't decide," I groaned. "They're all so cute!"

"Should we ask the Miacorns?" Briony said.

"Yes! Why didn't I think of that? We could do an Instagram poll and put all three of the dresses on hold. Then, I could come back in two days and buy the one the most people liked," I said. "It would be another way of, like, bringing my followers to the dance with me."

“Right,” joked Briony, “since you can’t exactly bring a million friends with you. And, actually, it was your mom’s idea. Remember yesterday, when she picked us up from the café and suggested you let the Miacorns help you pick your dress?”

“You’re right,” I said. “And, hey—she can vote, too!”

We laughed, and I changed back into each dress separately so Briony could snap photos. We also quickly checked with the store manager to make sure they’d hold all three dresses for me for forty-eight hours. I threw the pictures up on my Instagram stories one by one, then posted a poll asking the Miacorns to vote for their favorite dress. Ever since I’d done my first fan takeover on Instagram, I’d been asking my followers for more and more input. It felt like I had a ton of girlfriends with me, right there in the store.

“No matter which they choose, you’ll look gorgeous,” said Briony.

“I love yours, too,” I told her. “That color is beautiful!”

Briony linked her arm in mine. "We'll be the two belles of the ball!"

We giggled and strolled out of the store, feeling like two debutantes in an old movie.

Next, we were going to try and find some new shoes, then swing by Sephora to decide on some makeup looks. By the time we left the mall, we should have been completely ready for the dance! But we were barely out of the dress store when we heard someone call—

"Briony? Is that you?"

7

"Oh, my gosh," Briony whispered, grabbing my elbow hard. "Is that—"

"Hey! It *is* you! And the Famous Mia Fizz."

It was Liam, a boy at Briony's school who she had a *major* crush on. He wrote for the school newspaper and had written an article on the production of *A Midsummer Night's Dream* that Briony had directed. He'd even interviewed me. He was cute, and nice enough, but something about him had rubbed me the wrong way. It had felt like he was using Briony to get on my YouTube channel, and he'd seemed way more interested in *Mia's Life* than either me or Briony in *real* life. Still, he was Briony's crush—I owed it to her to give him a chance.

"Hi, Liam," I said.

"H-hi," Briony stuttered. She was super nervous—I sent her a mental BFF message to play it cool, but it didn't seem to make it to her brain. She was playing with her hair and fidgeting as if her favorite YouTuber,

Sofie Dossi, was standing in front of her. My cool, confident BFF turning into mush in front of a boy? That wasn't like her.

"I'm just here to get some new shoes," he said, flipping his hair out of his face. "What are you guys doing?"

"Finding dresses for—" I started, but Briony elbowed me. *Hard*.

"Ow," I hissed.

"Just...hanging out," Briony finished for me.

Liam nodded and turned to me. "Cool. Are you filming for your channel?"

I shook my head. "Not right this second." Liam was a male Miacorn—I did have a few guy followers. I figured he'd probably see the dresses on Instagram later, but I didn't want to make it seem like the only thing I ever did was create *Mia's Life* content.

"Well, good to see you guys," he said, turning away. Obviously, we weren't worth five minutes of conversation if my camera wasn't out. Whatevs. He ducked into the shoe store we were standing right outside of, and I turned to Briony, confused.

"Why couldn't I tell him about the dance?" I asked.

She shook her head. "I don't know! I just panicked. I didn't want him to, like, decide *he* was going to go or something. Or what if he thought it sounded dorky?"

I rolled my eyes. Who cared if someone thought something we were doing was dorky? We were excited about the dance, and that was all that mattered—not Liam's opinion. But, then, I had a great idea.

"Wait a second..." I shook my head. "Why *doesn't* he go? Oh, my gosh—duh! You should ask him!" She'd had a crush on Liam for ages. This was the perfect opportunity for her to make her move, just like I had with Finn.

Briony groaned. "It's not like I haven't thought about it. I'd *love* to have a date to the dance. Going as you and Finn's third wheel will be fun, but it might be awkward, too. I want a crush of my *own* on my arm."

"Well, he's right there!" I squealed. This was all going to work out perfectly!

"But..." she bit her lip. "What if he—"

I raised an eyebrow at her. "I *know* you're not about to say, '*what if he says no?*' Isn't that exactly what I asked you about asking Finn? And you told me that *we'd* go to the dance together no matter what and just forget we ever met him. We'll do the exact same thing if Liam says no."

"It's different, Mia. We go to the same school. I have to see him every single day!"

I shook my head. "Aren't you always telling me I need to be bold? Well, this is your chance. Just imagine it—walking in with Liam on your arm. Maybe even getting to slow dance! It would be so magical. Are you really going to risk even the possibility of going with him because you're too chicken?"

She winced. "When you put it that way..."

I nodded confidently. "It's my duty as your bestie

to insist you walk into that shoe store, shoulders back, and ask that boy to the dance. Like, *now*."

Briony opened her mouth as if to argue, but, just as quickly, she shut it, turned on her heel, and marched into the store.

I grinned. My BFF points today had to be through the roof!

8

I stood back and watched Briony tap Liam on the shoulder. When he turned around, she started talking, and I could tell she was inviting him to the dance. I was so proud of her! Asking a guy in person was a whole new level. At least with my text to Finn, I hadn't had to look him in the eyes.

But, suddenly, I started to worry. As Liam responded, his eyes were kind of glancing around—he looked nervous. Then, I saw Briony's face fall a little bit. Uh-oh. Things didn't seem to be going well. Was this a mistake? Maybe I shouldn't have pushed so hard.

Briony turned to head back to me, and I knew what

had happened instantly. Her eyes were tearing up, and Liam was trying to look busy on his phone.

"Come on," I whispered, grabbing her arm. "This calls for french fries."

Even through her tears, Briony giggled a little. "Is that your BFF-got-rejected-and-is-humiliated emergency snack?"

"It is now," I said.

After I'd ordered us two huge plates of fries, we sat in the food court, and Briony walked me through the conversation. Apparently, she'd explained about the dance to Liam and asked him to go as her date. But he'd said he didn't like her in that way, so he didn't think it would be fair to her to say yes.

"It was *so* embarrassing," she said. "I'm going to have to see him in school tomorrow, and it's going to be awkward. I'm totally going to avoid him in the hallways. But we have a few classes together."

I winced. Part of me wished I had never suggested

Briony ask him.. But, as if she could read my mind, she shook her head.

"It's not your fault, Mia. I did the same thing to you.

And everything you said was true—if he had said yes, it would have been worth the risk. Best friends are *supposed* to help you do scary things. It's just hard to see that right this second."

"Of course it is," I told her. "I don't blame you at all. I think it was *so* brave of you to ask him, and I'm glad you did. Besides..." I hesitated.

"Besides what?" she asked.

I took a deep breath. Should I tell her? Well, she couldn't really be any more upset than she was now.

"I never really liked him!" It burst out of me. "You're way too good for that guy. I mean, I know he's a Miacorn, but he had such an attitude. I know there's a guy out there for you who's sweet and kind and a ton of fun. *Not* obsessed with YouTube stardom."

To my surprise, Briony cracked up.

"I mean, he had a good side," she said. "But...He *was* always looking at his phone. He gets it confiscated at school, like, every single day."

"See?" I said.

"Plus, one time I caught him writing his own name

in his notebook over and over. He said he was practicing his autograph."

The two of us laughed so loudly people actually turned to look at us.

"And, hey—at least he was honest," I told her. "I mean, if he was a *giant* jerk, he would have said yes just to be featured on *Mia's Life*. Now you don't need to waste your time on somebody who isn't worth it."

"That's true," said Briony, wiping away her tears. Now, half were from the rejection and half were from giggling so hard. "But still. The dance is going to be way less fun now."

"Hey! You're still going with me," I reminded her.

"Yeah, you and *Finn*. Don't get me wrong—I'm totally happy for you! But it's going to be you two on a date and me just…hanging out. Maybe I just shouldn't go at all. I bet I have thirty days to return that dress."

"Absolutely not," I said firmly. "You are coming with me. You're the one who was there when I found the flyer, and you're the person I have the most fun with in the entire world. If it wasn't for you, I never would have even had the courage to text Finn! You *have* to come. And, if I start to exclude you or leave you feeling left out, just say…I don't know. A code word."

"Banana split," she said.

"Perfect," I said. "Just say banana split, and I'll make sure to hang out with you more."

"Well, I still want you and Finn to have an amazing time. You *better* slow dance with him—at least once," Briony insisted. "And hey, who knows? Maybe there'll be a boy there I meet on the dance floor."

"That's the spirit," I said with a grin. "And even if there's not, we're going to have an amazing time."

"Promise?" she asked.

"Promise," I swore.

9

The week flew by as I juggled school, my YouTube channel, and dance preparation. I'd mapped out the content for *Mia's Life*, and I was excited to make a video featuring different looks the Miacorns could rock at a school dance. Sienna was helping me, too—I was trying really hard to include her after I'd shot down her Pinterest boards. We decided that, on Wednesday, we'd do a few different looks and film them together.

"Only T-minus three days till the dance," I told my camera as I spread foundation on my face. "So, today, I'm going to help you guys put together a few different looks. The first is going to be a really natural, laid-back, California-girl style, if you're not looking to get super fancy. The next is a bit more glam and upscale. That's what I'm going to do for the actual dance on Saturday, since I've never been to a dance before. I just really want to go all out!"

I walked my viewers through the different types of makeup I was putting on, from some shimmery lip gloss to the newest shade of eyeliner I was digging. You wouldn't believe how tricky it is to talk *while* doing your makeup! For my more natural look, I just wore my hair in a long braid. Sienna came in to do my hair, and we giggled to the camera while she perfected her french-braiding skills. I had a *lot* of hair to work with, so braiding my hair was quite the project.

"And there you have it!" I said happily. "This is look number one." I paused, knowing right there, I'd put a *before* photo in so the Miacorns could see the total transformation. "This is the perfect look for a more casual dance where you're just going to wear jeans and a cute shirt—where you want to look cute, but not *too* fancy. Next, we're going to do our glam look." I leaned over and turned off the camera.

"Whew," I said. Even though I was used to making videos for *Mia's Life*, it was still pretty tiring to create an entire makeup and hair look, only to have to wash it off and start again.

"You look great, but who would wear something so simple to a dance?" Sienna asked.

I laughed. "Plenty of people! Not everyone loves all of the glitz and glam. A lot of different people watch the channel...I like to do something for everyone!"

"Well, I'm way more excited about *this* look," said Sienna, pointing to the inspiration pictures we'd printed out. We were going to practice the big curls look we'd decided on for my hair, and my makeup was going to be bolder, too.

After I'd scrubbed my face clean and done another intro, I started on my new makeup look. I explained to my viewers why I loved highlighter, the importance of finding the right lip gloss color, and why waterproof mascara rocks. Some people would probably have been embarrassed to show their bare, makeup-free face on YouTube, but not me. Even though I did a lot of beauty content, I always wanted the Miacorns to know they didn't have to be afraid of acne or redness. I mean, come on—we were teenagers! These things were going to happen. You could be proud of your natural skin *and* like playing with blush.

"Now, that's what I'm talking about!" said Sienna, plugging in the curling iron. A brand had sent it to me ages ago, but I didn't really use it too much. "You look so, so gorgeous."

I laughed. "Thanks. Ready for my hair?"

"Totally. I've been watching a ton of videos on curling techniques," she promised.

Sienna waved to the camera, and I explained what she was about to do.

"So, first you spray your hair with hair spray,"

Sienna explained. "A lot of people want to do it after, but, actually, too much spray can weigh your hair down. So, if you have hair that needs a lot of help to hold a curl, like Mia's, you want to spray each section *before* you curl it." She demonstrated with the spray before walking the Miacorns through the right way to wrap the hair around the curling iron and rotate it away from your face.

"Perfect," I told her. "Now, you can just do the rest, and I'll play it speeded up." That was one of my favorite video techniques—playing things quickly with some fun music in the background. Viewers didn't have to watch every strand of hair on my head get curled! And, besides, the process was probably going to take a while. It would be better to find a great song and let everyone watch the process speeded up x4.

"Sounds good," she said, wrapping another section of my hair around the curling iron.

"I'm glad you're helping me," I told her. "This is fun."

She grinned. "Thanks for *letting* me help. I feel like,

by the time I'm old enough to go to a dance, I'll be a pro at hair care." We laughed.

"Well, I hope you find a guy as great as Finn to go with," I said happily. "I can't wait to see him Saturday!"

"Mia?" she said. "Can I ask you something?"

"You just did," I joked.

"I mean it," she giggled. "What's it—what's it feel like, to have a crush? Like, how did you *know* you liked Finn?"

Hmm. I thought for a moment. How *did* I know I liked Finn? I thought back to when I had first met him at the community center.

"Well," I admitted. "First, I just thought he was cute. He caught my eye. But cuteness only goes so far. There are a lot of good-looking people you wouldn't want to spend a lot of time with." I thought of Liam. He may have looked great on the outside, but, on the inside, I had a feeling he was kind of a jerk. Just like how brands could send me fun hair products or vegan snacks in cute, colorful packages—it didn't necessarily mean I'd like what was inside them!

"So, how did you decide you wanted to spend time with him?" she asked.

"You know when you have a shirt that just seems to fit perfectly?" I asked. "You pull it on, and you feel really comfortable, and you also like how you look in the mirror? You almost feel like it impacts you. You might be more organized or energetic or just...confident. You feel *right* in it. Do you know what I mean?"

"That's how I feel when I wear my cat ears," Sienna said.

I laughed. "It's kind of the same thing as a crush. That boost you get from wearing your cat ears is the boost I get from being around Finn. Or even thinking about him! I just like who I am when I'm with him. And I think about him *all* the time. Like, someone could say they like chocolate, and I'd instantly think about how Finn loves chocolate! It's kind of ridiculous."

"Kind of," Sienna said. "But it also sounds fun. I can't wait to have a crush. All of the boys I know are..." she wrinkled her nose.

"I used to think like that, too," I said. "But you'll see. One day a guy will just catch your eye, and, before you know it, you're crushing. You don't need to think about it too much. You have a lot of time before you need to find a guy. We both do! Maybe the dance is the only date I ever go on with Finn. I'm still excited, and I know it'll be fun."

It was so cute that Sienna looked up to me, but I knew it was a big responsibility, too. She could learn a lot from books, movies, or even YouTube channels. But what her big sister said and did was always going to have the biggest influence on her.

She sighed. "Ugh. I'm so jealous."

"Don't be jealous," I told her. "You're going to have a crush of your own one day. I just know it! Maybe he'll even be into all things outer space, like you!"

She grinned. "You should really be thanking *me* for liking all things outer space. If I didn't like space, you wouldn't have decided on space camp for my birthday gift. And, if I didn't go to space camp, you never would have seen the flyer for the dance!"

"Speaking of the dance," I said nervously, "how's my hair looking?" We were sitting in front of my computer, so I didn't have a mirror. I hoped it was turning out okay.

Suddenly, Sienna jumped. "Oh, no!" she shrieked.

What?!

Not a good sign!

Not a good sign at *all!*

10

"What do you mean, oh, no?!" I asked, panic in my voice. Then I realized: there was the smell of burnt hair in the air.

My burnt hair!

"Sienna!" I shrieked. I grabbed the side of my head that she'd been working on, trying to feel for where the burned pieces were.

She started speaking really fast. "Okay, okay, okay. We can fix this. I can just—I can make this right. All we need to do is..."

But I realized what she'd done as she pulled the curling iron away from my head. There was an entire ringlet of hair, *my* hair, hanging from it. She'd gotten so distracted thinking about crushes that she'd literally burned off a chunk of my hair! The entire room smelled like a fire.

I jumped up and ran into the bathroom, my sister calling after me. Thank goodness we weren't livestreaming!

"Wait! Mia!" called Sienna. "I can fix it. I mean, I think it just makes you look more edgy. It's...different! Unique! It's still really pretty!"

But, as soon as I saw myself in the mirror, my jaw dropped. Sienna had burned off at least three inches of a section of my hair—right by my face! It didn't look edgy; it looked like I'd gotten in a fight with some scissors and lost. Or like I'd tried to hack a DIY haircut and completely failed. It was horrible!

My eyes welled up with tears. Part of me felt like it was silly to be so upset about something like a hairdo. But I had really been looking forward to the dance and getting to go with Finn. How I looked mattered to me. I wanted to be confident and cute and not worry about how ridiculous my hair looked. All of my hopes for a great look flew out the window. Finn probably wouldn't even want to be seen with me. Any pictures we took would always remind me of how bad my hair looked. You could cover up a pimple with makeup, but your hair? It's not like I could go out and buy a wig! This was terrible, and there was nothing I could do to make it better. I wanted to curl up in a ball in my bedroom and never come out again.

"Girls?" Mom appeared suddenly, Koa on her hip. His eyes were wide. "Is everything okay? I thought you were working on your video, but I heard a lot of commotion."

"No," I said through my tears, "everything is *not* okay!"

Sienna came out of my room nervously. "I kind of... messed up Mia's hair a little..."

"A little?!" I yelled. "Mom, look!" I pointed to where she'd burned off a chunk of hair.

Mom gasped. "That's what that smell was! Thank goodness. I thought you two had knocked over a candle or something."

I tried to take a deep breath and exhale slowly, like my favorite meditation app taught me. "Mom. Focus. Sienna burned off a chunk of my hair. I look terrible. I'm going to the dance in three days, and my hair looks awful. She said she was going to help me, not ruin how I looked."

"It was an accident," insisted Sienna. "I'm really sorry!"

"*Sorry* doesn't bring back my hair," I snapped.

"Girls," Mom said, "Fighting isn't going to solve the problem. Now, Mia, I'm sure we can make an appointment to get your hair fixed somehow."

"How?" I snapped. I didn't usually talk to my family like that unless it was on a dare for a YouTube video. But I was mad—*really* mad. "They can only cut hair *off* at a salon, not make it grow back! This is all my fault. I shouldn't have let Sienna help. She's too young, and her head is always in the clouds."

"That's not fair," said Sienna, her lip quivering. Now *she* was near tears. "I didn't mean to do it, honest. I just wanted to help."

"Well, you didn't help, did you?" I said. "I know you didn't mean to, Sienna. You're just a little kid. But, if you can't handle the responsibility of paying attention to a curling iron, you can't handle the responsibility of helping with my channel! From now on, I'm doing everything myself. I do *not* want your help...ever again!"

Now, Sienna was really crying. But I didn't care. Something inside me had snapped. I stormed out of the bathroom, ran back into my bedroom, and slammed the door as hard as I could. Then I flung myself onto my bed and burst into tears.

11

After about ten minutes, there was a soft knock on my door.

"Mia?" Mom asked. "Can I come in?"

"Sure," I mumbled into my pillow, wiping away the last of my tears. Part of me wanted to be alone, but Mom always made me feel better. Besides, she usually gave great advice.

Mom came in and sat down gently on the edge of my bed. "I can tell you're really upset."

I nodded. "I feel like the entire dance is ruined."

"Hmm. Is it, though? You're still going to look incredible—yes, I know, your hair isn't perfect, but there *are* solutions to be found. You're still going to go with your best friend and a boy you really like. You're still going to dance your butt off and have a terrific time. It doesn't sound ruined to me."

I thought about it for a minute. Now that I was calmer, I could see that Mom was obviously right. Going to the dance wasn't about how my hair looked. But it had just been so tempting to think I could make everything

perfect if I tried hard enough. I wanted everything to go according to plan, but it wasn't going to.

"Mia, I think you really hurt your sister's feelings, and that's the most important thing," Mom said kindly. "I completely understand that you're upset. Sienna should have been more focused. At the same time, she's younger than you. And you're her role model. Sienna's way of showing you how much she loves you is trying to be involved in your life—a big part of which is your channel. Even if she doesn't do it perfectly all the time, that's what she's trying to do. Part of being a good role model means demonstrating how to handle your anger and even offering forgiveness."

I sighed. I knew Mom was right. I couldn't believe some of the things I'd said to Sienna. I winced as I remembered telling her that her head was always in the clouds and that I didn't want her help anymore. Neither of those things were true. I'd just been *so* angry.

"I didn't mean to hurt her feelings," I said. "I just lost my temper."

"Just like she didn't mean to burn your hair. She just lost concentration," Mom pointed out.

"Fair," I admitted.

"Imagine someone you love and respect telling you the things you told to your sister," Mom said. "You'd be devastated."

"I know," I said.

"So, how do you think we could solve the problem?" Mom asked. "Because I have two very upset daughters." Downstairs, we heard Dad yell "Karma, no!" and then something crashed to the floor. My youngest sister started crying, too.

"Make that three," Mom said. I couldn't help it—I started giggling, and so did she.

"I think I need to apologize to Sienna," I said. Sometimes it was hard having a family that was so close. My sister and I were both homeschooled, so we spent a *lot* of time together. That meant she saw all the sides of me—my good and bad! But I knew I was lucky to have a sibling who wanted to be part of my world so badly. Sienna could be exhausting, but, at the end of the day, I was the older one. I had to set the example, and I probably always would. Even when we were in our nineties, I'd be giving her life advice, and she'd be driving me to distraction.

"I think you're right," Mom replied. "And I think *I* need to go help your dad with the babies downstairs."

I gave Mom a big hug and went to go knock on Sienna's bedroom door.

12

"Sienna?"

"Go away!"

I'd been knocking on my sister's door for at least five minutes, and I'd gotten nowhere. She didn't want anything to do with me. Was she going to stay angry forever?

"Sienna, I really need to talk to you," I said, trying to stay patient.

"Text me."

"No! I want to do it face-to-face," I said. "It's important." This wasn't the type of apology I could send over the phone. Besides, I wasn't about to text someone who was sitting five feet away from me!

I was just about to turn away—maybe she needed some space and leaving her alone would be the best choice after all. But, finally, I heard the lock on her bedroom door turn over.

I tentatively poked my head in. Sienna was throwing herself back on her bed after unlocking the door—it was almost funny how similar she looked to me just a few minutes ago. Her walls were decorated with posters of her favorite YouTube stars, and the twinkle lights she had wrapped around her bedposts were blinking on and off. We'd done a room makeover for her on the YouTube channel just a few months ago. The whole space screamed *Sienna*.

"Sienna," I said, "I'm really sorry. I completely lost my temper. I didn't mean what I said. Of *course* I want your help getting ready for the dance. I always want your help with *Mia's Life*. I know things have been a little bumpy lately, but I'm still figuring out how to run my channel while accepting help. You're my sister, and

I never want to make you upset or hurt your feelings. Do you forgive me?"

Sienna laid silently on her bed. I sighed—was she just going to be angry forever?

But finally, she rolled over and looked at me grumpily. "I guess I'm sorry, too."

"You are?"

"If I'm going to help with your channel, I need to be more focused and not goof off. I know I ruined your hair. And I feel really bad about it."

"Don't feel bad," I told her. "It was an accident. We can fix it somehow." I wasn't sure how much I believed that, but I had to hope it was true.

"You still want my help?" she asked in a small voice.

"Of course," I said confidently. "What's *Mia's Life* without you in it?"

She got off her bed and gave me a big hug. "Thanks, Mia."

I squeezed her extra tight. I hated being in a fight with

my sister, and I was glad it was over. But, even though I'd made up with Sienna, I still had a sinking feeling about the dance. What was I supposed to do now? How could I even finish the vlog we'd started making? Had I been right in the first place about burned hair being impossible to fix? I wasn't mad at Sienna anymore, but maybe her mistake *was* unfixable. Or maybe it was a sign that this whole royal ball idea was a bad one to begin with.

After Sienna went downstairs to find the rest of our family, I retreated to my room and pulled out my phone. I had to call my BFF.

"Thank you for saving me from math homework," Briony answered.

I laughed. "Anytime."

"What's up? Did you

make your big vlog with Sienna today?" Briony asked excitedly.

I paused. Where to even start? But, being my bestie, Briony could instantly tell something was up.

"Okay," she said. "Spill. What's wrong?"

I took a deep breath and started at the beginning—Sienna and me finding the photo for hair inspo, making the plan to practice it a few days in advance, and sitting down to make the vlog. I told Briony how Sienna had started asking me questions about what it was like to have a crush and how I'd started talking to her about Finn. When I got to the part about the burned hair, I heard her gasp.

"How much?" she asked.

"About three inches," I moaned. "Right by my face. You can't miss it—it's horrible. I'm not just being dramatic. It's really obvious."

"Oh, my gosh. That stinks! Did it hurt?"

"No," I told her. "I didn't even feel it. Then I totally

lost it on Sienna and exploded, telling her I didn't want her help anymore and that she was too young to be responsible."

"Wow," Briony said. "I bet that really upset her."

"It did. And I felt terrible, so I apologized. She said sorry, too. *We're* fine now. But my hair's still a mess, and I just..."

"You just what?"

I bit my lip. "I'm starting to wonder if this whole dance thing is such a good idea." I started twirling the end of my hair with my fingers, one of my nervous habits. But feeling how much shorter it was in the front made me upset all over again.

"Why do you say that?" asked Briony.

"I know it sounds dumb," I admitted. "But I don't want Finn to see me with my hair all messed up. And also, how am I supposed to show the Miacorns my dance look? I'm their *guide*. I do demonstrations on how to look and feel your best. Am I just supposed to show up and be like, oops, sometimes you accidentally burn three inches off your hair? My viewers would never trust me again. They'd think I had no idea what I was talking about. I really don't want to ditch Finn, but maybe if I played sick...I mean, he can't get mad at me for having a fever, right?"

"Mia!" Briony interrupted me. "Slow down. You're getting, like, twelve steps ahead."

"Ugh. Sorry."

"Okay," Briony said, "*First* of all, you're not the Miacorns' guide."

"I'm not?" I asked, confused.

"No!" she said. "You're more like...their adventure buddy. You're on the walk *with* them. You're learning things as you go, just like they are! That's why people like to follow you. If they wanted to see picture-perfect makeup looks, they could look at a celebrity who has an entire glam team and never posts anything about themselves that isn't perfect. How often are you talking about showing up as you are on social media? Showing photos of you without makeup and stuff? Telling the truth about awkward moments? You've never tried to be flawless before!"

"I know," I said. "That's true..."

"Well, I hate to call you out like this. But, as your BFF, I have to ask—do you mean it or not?" she said. Briony had a way of saying kinda harsh things in a super nice voice that made me feel empowered, not hurt. "Because it's one thing to talk the talk but another to walk the walk. I mean, what would you say to a Miacorn in your situation? Would you really say, 'You're right, your hair's a mess, so you should probably just sit at home and watch TV instead of having the night of your life'?"

I thought of all the times I'd shared embarrassing stories about my period or even talked about body odor and growing boobs to the Miacorns. Briony was right. I wasn't someone who had all the answers—I'd never pretended to be that person! I was a virtual friend who was sharing her experiences. That's all.

"I guess not going to the dance because I'm embarrassed about my hair would send the wrong message," I said. I didn't want my followers to think, just because they were having a bad hair day, they had to sit at home.

"Exactly," said Briony. "Anyway, you wouldn't just be ditching Finn. You'd be ditching me. After the Liam disaster, you can't expect me to go to the royal ball alone! You promised you'd be by my side and that we'd have an amazing time, crush or no crush. You can't back out now."

I laughed. "Okay! Okay. You're right. I would never leave you hanging like that." Pep talks from Briony were the best cure for a bad mood—or a bad hairdo.

"Besides," she said excitedly. "I think I have an idea on how to fix your hair."

"I'm all ears," I said. I caught a glance of myself in the mirror—my right ear was totally visible, now that my hair had been burned off. "Literally."

13

Briony's idea was five feet tall with spiky lime-green hair, giant glasses, and dangly earrings in the shape of kittens.

"I'm Tonya," she told me. "What the heck happened to you?"

Tonya was Briony's favorite stylist at Roots, where she always got her hair done. She'd assured me over and over that Tonya could fix *anything*. Briony had already made an appointment to get her own hair cut before the dance, so she'd called Tonya and begged to squeeze me in right before.

I grimaced. "It's rough, right? My little sister, a daydream, and a curling iron. Does that paint the picture?"

"Crystal clearly," she said, stepping back and narrowing her eyes at my head. I glanced at Briony nervously, but she just grinned back. I mean, I liked Tonya's green spikes on *her*, but she wasn't going to turn *me* lime-colored, was she?

"I can fix this," Tonya announced. "Sit." She pointed toward her style station, and I slid into the chair. I tried not to get dizzy from the overwhelming scent of hair dye, hair spray and conditioning product. I could barely hear anything over the noise of a million blow dryers.

For almost an hour, Tonya muttered to herself, washing my hair and carefully snipping the sides. I tried not to look in the mirror, and Briony distracted me by checking the results of the Instagram poll I'd posted on my dress.

"So far, the one in the lead is...Well, let's just see when they all come in," she told me. "There may be a last-minute surge."

"I hope it's the—ouch!" I winced, as Tonya yanked on my head a little too hard.

"Sorry," she murmured, not taking her eyes from my scalp. "Stay still, please."

I sighed, trying not to lose faith that my hair disaster could turn into something beautiful. I hadn't posted anything about my hair disaster yet, but I *had* let Briony snap a few photos to show the Miacorns later. *After* Tonya worked her magic, hopefully.

My phone buzzed, and Briony handed it back to me to see who it was.

"A text from Finn!" I squealed.

Only two more days—can't wait to rock the dance floor!

I turned the phone to show Briony. "Is *perfection* too strong a word?"

She laughed. "Well, I think we learned a thing or two about aiming for perfection this week. But he sure is cute. I love how excited he is—it's adorable."

"All right," Tonya said, confidently whipping off the smock I'd been wearing. "Voilà."

I squeezed my eyes shut. "I can't look. Briony, tell me—is it okay?"

"You're doubting my work?" asked Tonya, sounding offended.

"No!" I insisted. "I just—"

Briony laughed. "Mia! Open your eyes and look in the mirror."

I peeked my eyes open, but just a little at first. I caught a glimpse of a girl in the mirror with casual, breezy blond hair in fashionable layers.

Wait a second—that girl was me!

"Oh, my gosh!" I squealed. My hair didn't look like my little sister had burned it off. It looked like I'd gotten a chic new look!

"I *love* it!" I said happily. "I can't believe how great it looks. Oh, my gosh...I think it looks even better than it did before!"

Tonya smiled smugly. "That's what I do."

Briony elbowed me. "Told you it was fixable! I love how she did the layers in front. It's even, but not too wild, and it all flows to the back really nicely. It looks fashionable, not like...well, not like your sister burned your hair off with a curling iron."

I threw my arms around my BFF. "You were right, you were right, you were right. I'll say it a million times!"

“Three down, 999,997 to go,” she giggled. “Now move it—it’s my turn!”

After I waited for Briony to get her own Tonya-approved makeover, we went back to my house. Her hair was just as glamorous as mine—Tonya had added honey-colored highlights and done some layered framing right around her face. We were going to look fantastic at the ball.

“Hello?” I called out as we walked into the Fizz foyer. “Anybody home?”

Sienna came rushing downstairs, eager to see my new hairdo.

“Oh, my gosh!” she squealed. “Mia! It looks *amazing*. You can’t even tell I...”

“Burned my hair off?” I asked with a smirk.

She buried her face in her hands. “You aren’t still mad at me, are you?”

I laughed. “No! In fact, maybe you even did me a favor. I *love* my new hair!”

"Briony, you look fantastic, too," Mom said happily, walking into the foyer with Dad, Karma, and Koa. "You two are going to be the prettiest girls there!"

"Well, we'll have the best hair, at least," Briony said. "Thank you, Tonya!"

"Thank you, Briony," I told her, throwing my arm around her. "If it wasn't for you, I'd be plotting out my stay-home-sick plan of attack as we speak."

"Well, if it wasn't for *you*, I wouldn't be going at all, after Liam turned me down," Briony said with a wince.

"These new haircuts call for pizza," Dad announced. "Who's in?"

"Me!" we all said unanimously.

Just then, my phone buzzed again.

"Another text from Finn?" Briony asked excitedly.

I glanced at the screen. "No! It's my poll results. The Miacorns picked my dress!"

14

"It's the blue and white one!" I said happily. I was excited. Pink may have been my go-to color, but I *loved* the dress they chose.

"That's going to look great, Mia," Mom said. "Should we run to the mall and pick it up? Then we can snag our pizza on the way home."

"I should get going, actually," Briony said. "I totally forgot I have a major math test tomorrow. And if I skip studying because I'm getting ready for a dance, my mom and dad are *not* going to be thrilled."

"We'll drop you off on the way," Mom said.

After I waved goodbye to Briony—and thanked my lucky stars for homeschooling yet again, because a math test sounded horrible—Mom, Sienna, and I headed to the mall. Dad had stayed back with Koa and Karma to make a side salad for our pizza dinner.

"Now, you've got your hair *and* your dress figured out," said Sienna. "Your makeup's going to look great, too. Your whole look is complete!"

"It's starting to feel really...real. The dance is only two days away," I said. "Let's hope my dress is still on hold!"

Thankfully, it was. The cashier happily pulled my dress out, and I remembered how much I loved the soft fabric and the way the skirt swung and shimmered. I tried it on again to make sure it fit and had Sienna take a quick Boomerang clip that I could post on Instagram.

That night, after we'd stuffed ourselves on vegan pizza, I was trying to catch up on some reading when Sienna knocked on my door.

"Hey," she said. "Are you planning out *Mia's Life* stuff?"

"Nope," I said, holding up my book. "Just trying to get some schoolwork done, actually."

She came and sat on the edge of my bed. "I'm glad we made up from our fight."

"Me too," I said. "I really do appreciate all your help with the channel. You know that, right?"

She nodded. "And I think your viewers picked the perfect dress. It looks like it just makes you feel more *you*. Kinda like...what we were talking about earlier? With your crush? It just *fits* right."

I grinned. "Exactly. But I'd pick Finn over a cute dress any day!"

"But you didn't pick the dress! The Miacorns did," joked Sienna. "Would you do a poll to let them pick your crush?"

"Definitely not," I responded. "*But*... I would take advice from people around me who I knew and trusted. If Briony thought something was off about Finn, I'd want to know. And you know I'd always do that for you, right? If you need help deciding if a crush is for you or not, we can always talk about it."

"Thanks, Mia," said Sienna. "And... I really am sorry about your hair."

"Don't be," I said, glancing in the mirror. "I think it all worked out in the end! And you *are* going to help me get ready on Saturday, right?"

"You still want me to?" Sienna asked, surprised. "I thought you'd never want me near your hair again!"

"Well...Maybe I can handle the hair, and you can help me with my makeup. With *guidance*," I reminded her.

"Deal. Thanks for the second chance."

"We're sisters," I said. "You'll never run out of chances with me!"

15

Finally, it was Saturday—the day of the dance!

I ran through my mental checklist in my head. DIY manicure? Check. Strapless bra fresh from the laundry? Check. Dress hanging in my closet? Check.

I was just about to have Sienna come in my room and help with my makeup, and then we'd tag team my hair. Then, Briony and Finn would be coming over, and we'd all head straight to the royal ball together. I knew my mom was going to want to take a thousand photos; plus, I was bringing my own phone to film some things for the vlog.

But, before it was time to go, I wanted to take a minute and make a video for the Miacorns. I knew I was going to make a video to show them how I looked before the dance and what I was wearing. But, first, I had another topic in mind.

I powered up my camera.

"Hello, Miacorns, and welcome back to *Mia's Life*!" I said happily. "Today, I just wanted to have a little chat and talk to you about something that's been on my mind lately, and that's...sibling relationships."

Part of me was nervous to share about what I'd experienced with Sienna that week. What if my viewers thought I was a total jerk? Would they unsubscribe because they didn't see me as nice anymore? But, at the end of the day, it was like Briony had said: if I was going to talk the talk, I had to walk the walk. I had learned something important that week through a mistake, and I knew it was something I could share with the Miacorns. After all, they weren't just followers—they felt like friends. And I didn't want to be the kind of vlogger that pretended to be perfect and only showed

up when things were neat, clean, and airbrushed. I wanted to share all of the parts of my life, even the ones that were a little more complicated. Even if I decided to keep some things off camera, it couldn't be because I was embarrassed of showing up as myself.

"This week, when I told Sienna about the dance, she was super excited. I mean, *just* as excited as I am! We've both seen dances in movies, but we never thought we'd really have the chance to go to one. So she wanted to help out...a lot. And you guys know my family is really close. Sienna is one of my best friends. We do everything together. Of course I wanted to let her help and feel like she was a part of things. But I learned pretty quickly that her idea of what would look fantastic and mine were just a little different. Not better or worse, just *different*."

I cringed a little, thinking of Sienna's original Pinterest boards. Then I remembered how much time she had probably put into them. And hey—there were people out there who would totally rock those wacky hairdos!

"I had a hard time explaining to her that her vision just wasn't what I was going for. So we teamed up and found a really gorgeous hairdo online. She even helped me put all of the curls in—it took ages. I was going to make a vlog for you guys all about it, but then an accident happened. We were talking, we *both* got distracted, and a chunk of my hair got burned off! Can you believe it?"

I almost had to laugh. My viewers knew how accident-prone I was. But burning off my hair felt like a whole new level!

"I got angry at Sienna. Really, *really* angry. And I said some hurtful things. We had a huge fight, we were both crying...It was a big deal. But, after I got all of my tears out, I realized something important. Sienna is my sister. Does that mean she's always right or that she never makes mistakes? Heck, no! My hair really did look terrible. But it *does* mean that she is worthy of my kindness. She's way more important than a hairdo. In fact, she's way more important than the entire dance itself. Plus, my BFF pointed out to me that I would never tell a Miacorn that, if her hair looked terrible, she should just sit at home and skip the dance. I would tell her that your hair might be fun and might give you confidence, but it's one of the least important parts of you! That being said, I was lucky enough to snag a spot with a great stylist who totally fixed my hair. Whew!"

I took a deep breath.

"So, what I'm trying to say is, remember this: sibling relationships can be complicated. They aren't always easy, even if you're close. But, if you put your priorities in the right order, you'll find out that even the biggest fights can all work out in the end. And, hey—if you burn your hair off, it's fixable."

I reached over and turned off the camera. I felt good about my message.

"Mia, that was so sweet," a voice said. I whipped my head around. Standing there was Mom, her hand over her heart, and behind her was Sienna, who was beaming.

"I meant every word," I said.

"I'm glad that I can still help with the channel," she said. "I promise—no daydreaming while holding hot objects ever again."

"Well, get in here," I said. "It's time to do my makeup!"

As I got ready, Sienna and I filmed every aspect of my look, from her careful (focused!) application of my makeup to the best way to get curls to stick. I showed off my dress before slipping it on and even showed the shoes I was going to pair with it. The Miacorns would have enough dance inspiration to last them a lifetime!

The doorbell rang, and I hurried to answer it. It was Briony, looking absolutely amazing in her emerald dress and gorgeous updo.

"You girls look straight out of a castle," Dad said, snapping photos as we posed cheesily. "You really nailed your looks!"

"I just hope Finn thinks so," I confessed.

"He does," someone behind me said. I turned around so fast I was surprised I didn't get whiplash—in fact, I'm pretty sure some of my curls did accidentally whack Briony in the face. Standing there was Finn, in a perfectly fitting suit, carrying a small flower.

"My stepsister said it's called a corsage," he said, sounding embarrassed. "For your wrist?"

"Oh, my gosh," I said. "Thanks! And, um—hi! Come on in!"

Briony pinched my arm, and I batted her hand away. But she was right. He looked adorable, from head to toe.

Finn stepped into the house, and I willed the rest of my family to play it cool. Koa pointed excitedly to the pretty white flower corsage as Finn slid it onto my wrist.

"How did you know my dress was blue and white?" I asked. "Oh, duh—Instagram!"

"Actually," Finn said as he winked at Sienna, "I may have had a little help."

My sister and I grinned at each other. I knew she'd always be on my team!

16

"By the way," Finn told me as we hopped out of my dad's car, "I love your new hair." I felt my cheeks get warm. I'd been hoping he'd notice! I hadn't posted the video yet that explained the hair fiasco, so he had no idea Sienna had gone all pyromaniac with the curling iron.

The community center had a huge banner hanging across the front door, reading "Welcome to the Royal Ball!" We made our way to the gym, and, once we stepped inside, it was like we'd stepped into a castle.

Everywhere we looked, we saw girls in gorgeous gowns and guys in suits like Finn's. There was a long white table on one end with the gym filled with chips, brownies, and bowls of punch. There was a huge

floral display in the middle of the room. Delicate strings of twinkle lights hung from the ceiling, and a band, similarly decked out in royalcore clothes, was rocking out on a makeshift stage at the front of the stage. A ton of people were dancing.

"This is incredible!" said Briony. "Oh, my gosh, look—a photo booth!" I turned to see where she was pointing. A photographer in a pink dress was snapping photos of people as they held up masquerade masks and crowns. They posed next to a couple of thrones.

"Wow," I said. "It definitely doesn't look like the community center anymore."

"Well, I guess there's only one way to kick this party off," said Finn. "Let's dance!"

I'd never danced so much in my life! Finn, Briony, and I jammed out to all kinds of songs that the band was playing—some more old-school, but some more current, too. We sang along if we knew the words. After a while, all three of us were hot and tired, so we went to grab some punch.

"What's a razzleberry?" Briony asked, wrinkling her nose.

"Who knows?" I said, chugging mine. "But it tastes good!"

"Hear ye, lords and ladies," the main singer said into the microphone. He was walking the line between being in character and being a total cheeseball, but I had to admit, he definitely gave the whole dance the "royal ball" vibes! "We're gonna slow this next one down a bit. Grab a partner and get cozy." The guitarist played a few slow chords, and I realized—it was the first slow song!

Finn turned to me, but, before he had a chance to ask me to dance, I grabbed Briony's arm.

"Don't you wish they had *banana splits* here?" I asked.

She looked at me, confused. She'd forgotten our code word! Then, I saw it click, and she grinned.

"Nope," she said. "No banana splits for me! Why don't you two go dance? I'm beat."

"Want to, um. I mean—would you like to—if you *want*, we could maybe..." Finn gestured toward the dance floor.

OMG! He was *nervous!*

"Sure," I said happily. The two of us headed out on the dance floor and started swaying back and forth. I couldn't believe it! My very first slow dance! What were we supposed to talk about? Wait, *were* we supposed to talk? Should I look him in the eyes? He had his hands on my hips, and I had mine around his shoulders. It wasn't like there were many other places to look!

"I'm really glad you invited me," Finn told me.

"Me too," I told him earnestly.

"And," he said, "I've been really having fun getting to know you lately. I had no idea that the cute girl at rock-climbing class would turn out to be so funny and smart."

Okay, now I was *definitely* blushing. Good thing I'd

worn the blue dress instead of the pink—my face would have matched my skirt!

"I've had fun getting to know you, too," I told him. "Really. And I'm happy you said yes to coming. It's been nice to spend some time thinking about someone other than my YouTube viewers."

"Well, I'm one of those, too," he laughed. "I never miss an episode of *Mia's Life*! Will I make the next episode?"

I grinned. "We'll have to see!"

But that did remind me—I'd hardly filmed anything for the channel! After our dance, Finn joined me as I hit *record* on my phone and showed the Miacorns some of the dance decorations on Instagram Live. I even swung the phone to Finn and let him wave hi for a second! And then, I saw someone in the background, standing just a bit behind Finn.

It was Briony! Oh, no—I should have found her right after the slow dance. But she wasn't alone. She was talking to a guy!

I quickly turned the camera back on myself and said goodbye to the Miacorns before ending the Live.

"Finn!" I hissed. "Look! Briony's talking to a boy."

He glanced at who he was, then grinned.

"That's not just any guy," he said. "That's Diego! He goes to my school. Diego!" he called out before I could stop him.

The guy who was talking to Briony—Diego, apparently—turned and waved to Finn. Briony made eye contact with me and sent me a BFF message with her eyes. *OMG!*

Finn and I walked over, and the boys started talking about soccer.

"He just came over and introduced himself," Briony mumbled to me quietly. "He's really nice."

"That's awesome," I whispered back. "Do you want to come hang out with me and Finn, or are you good here?"

"I'm fine here. I'll find you if I need you," she said.

I grabbed Briony's hand and squeezed it. Seriously—where would I be without my bestie? She seemed so much more confident with Diego than she ever had with Liam!

After Finn and Diego chatted for a minute, I pulled Finn back over to the snack table to give Briony and Diego some space.

"He's a nice guy at school, right? Not a creep or anything?" I asked Finn.

"Diego? He's awesome! He's the kind of guy who's nice to *everybody*. He walks down the hall and, like, everyone knows his name. But not because he's super popular. He's just a great dude."

I grinned. He sounded like the perfect guy for Briony to spend some time chatting with!

"So," I said, "are you up for another round on the dance floor?"

He grabbed my hand. "You read my mind!"

17

The rest of the dance, I felt like I was floating on a cloud. I spent hours dancing with Finn, goofing off with Briony, and drinking the delicious punch. Briony and Diego danced together a few times, and they even friended each other on Snapchat before we left. I couldn't wait to do a total debrief with her, but I wanted to wait until we were alone to do it. No offense to Finn—but some conversations were for BFF ears only!

Mom picked us up when the night was finally over, and, to my surprise, Sienna was in the front seat!

"Your hair held *perfectly*," was the first thing she said to me as we got in the car. "I told you the curls would work!"

I giggled.

"Thanks, Sienna. You were right!"

"You three look exhausted. Did you have fun?" Mom asked.

"It was a blast," Finn said. "I must have thanked Mia a million times for inviting me."

"It was just like the movies, only way, way better," I confirmed.

"Way more fun than my school dance," said Briony.

"I can't believe it's already over! It does feel good to get these shoes off, though."

Mom dropped Finn off, and he promised to text me the next day. As soon as he got out of the car, Mom, Sienna, and Briony all turned and grinned at me, wide-eyed.

"Yes, we slow danced," I laughed.

"I knew it!" squealed Sienna. "OMG, Mia, tell us *everything*."

"Briony has good news, too," I sang, bumping my shoulder into hers.

She blushed. "Let's just say I did *not* see that coming! Do you think he liked me?"

"Definite crush potential," I said confidently.

"Well, I'm glad you girls had such a terrific time," Mom said. "But it's getting late, and we're already on Briony's street. She'll have to fill us in another day."

Briony opened the car door and hopped out. But, before closing the door, she turned to me and winked.

"Thanks for not serving up too many banana splits," she said.

I smiled. "Any time."

The next day, with a face scrubbed free of dance makeup and my hair hanging down my back, I winced.

"Anything goes?" I asked excitedly.

"No cutting, and *no* burning," Sienna reminded me. "Besides that...anything goes!" I turned to the camera and made an *eek* face. Sienna was paying me back for the hair fiasco by letting me give her a totally out-of-this-world hairdo for the vlog! I'd found a picture on Pinterest of a girl with space buns all over her head, plus one long braid going down the back. She looked ridiculous—it would be perfect for goofy Sienna!

"But, after this, you can no longer be mad that I sort of ruined the dance for you," Sienna reminded me.

I laughed. "Ruined the dance? No way! The dance was one of the best nights I've ever had. We had so

F3 F4 F5 F6 F7 F8
W E R T Y U

much fun, and I got to hang out with Finn and Briony, and I loved my hair."

"I'm glad you had such a good time," she said. "Will this new look be dance-ready?"

"Well," I said, winking at the camera, "we'll have to see about that."

At the end of the day, I knew going to the dance was about so much more than hair. It was about trying new things, putting myself out there, and having fun with the people I loved. A great haircut and a pretty dress definitely didn't hurt. But a hair crisis—or a sister fight—couldn't ruin anything. I loved being Mia Fizz, YouTube star. But, even more than that, I loved being Mia Fizz, Sienna's big sister. And *that* was worth more than any haircut in the world!

ABOUT THE AUTHOR

Mia Fizz is a seventeen-year-old social media star with more than one million subscribers on her YouTube channel (*Mia's Life*). She's been featured in numerous magazines, has written multiple Amazon-bestselling books, and has appeared in a sold-out live show alongside her family. When not featuring on her family's YouTube channel (*Family Fizz*, which has more than two million subscribers), she likes to cook, practice Spanish, rock climb, and draw.